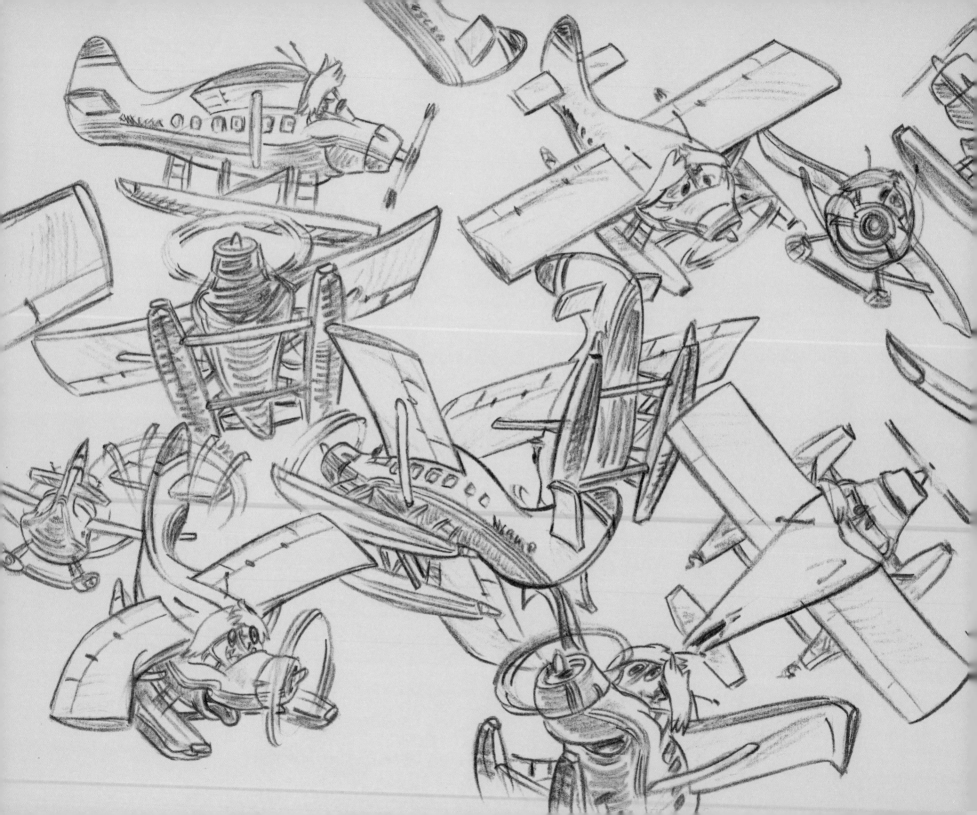

—First Edition—

Written by Kirk Thomas

Designed and Illustrated by
Gita Lloyd and Gasper Vaccaro

Since 1978

www.grandpasairplane.com

Printed in China.
Library of Congress Catalog Card Number: 2008925764
ISBN 978-1-59433-079-7

We live in Alaska.

There are lots and lots
of airplanes in Alaska.

Airplanes are used for many things. Grandpa has an airplane and he uses it for many things too.

Grandpa's airplane is an Otter but we just call it Grandpa's airplane. Grandpa's airplane has floats so it can land on water.

Some people call Grandpa a bush pilot but we just call him

Grandpa.

When we hear
Grandpa's airplane,
we always look up and say...

"There goes Grandpa."

Since Grandpa's airplane is a great big Otter, he hauls many people and lots of things to many different places.

Some days he has lots of trips. Every time he takes off we say...

"There goes

Grandpa."

Sometimes Grandpa brings people to town so they can go shopping or see a doctor.

Sometimes he takes food
and parts to fishing boats.

If someone gets hurt,
Grandpa picks them
up and takes them to
the hospital. Whenever
he flies by, we always say...

"There goes

Grandpa."

If someone gets lost in the wilderness—Grandpa goes with his airplane to find them.

They call it search and rescue, and the lost people are always happy when Grandpa finds them.

In Alaska, schoolkids travel to other towns for sports and other activities. When they need to travel, they ask

Grandpa to take them in his airplane because there are no roads. Whenever he goes by, we always say...

"There goes

Grandpa."

When visitors come to
Alaska as tourists, Grandpa
takes them on flightseeing trips

to show them beautiful
mountains and lakes.

Sometimes visitors want to see wild animals, so Grandpa tries to find bears or

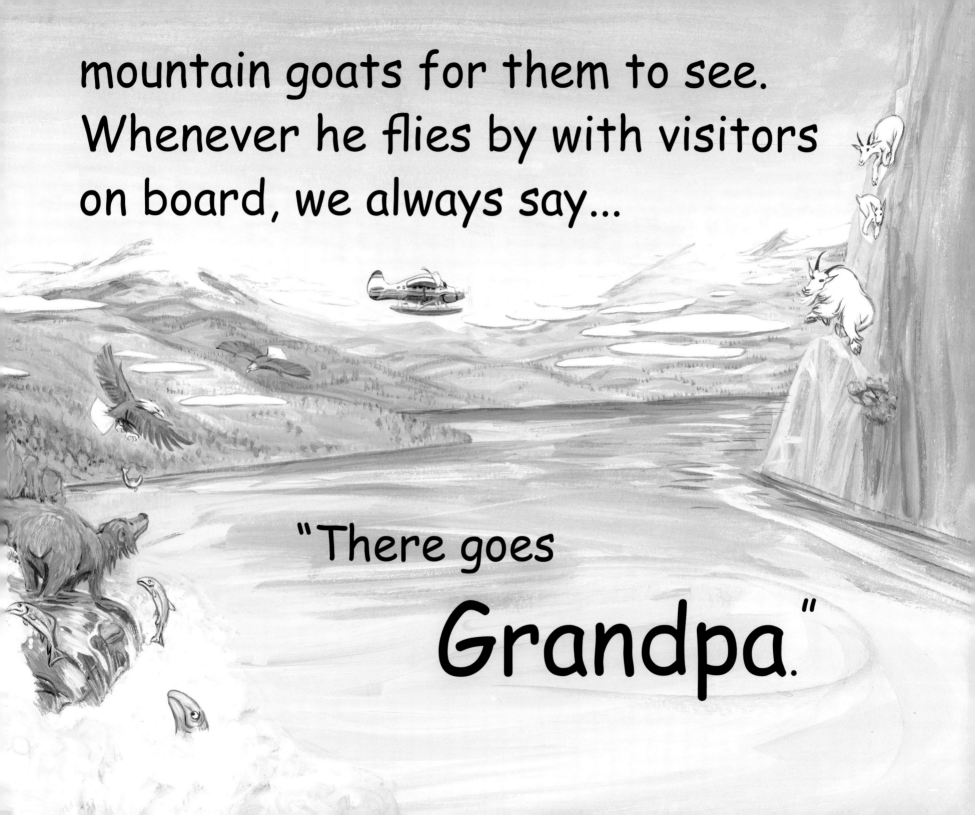

mountain goats for them to see. Whenever he flies by with visitors on board, we always say...

"There goes Grandpa."

Lots of people come to Alaska to go fishing. Grandpa loads them in his airplane and takes them to their favorite fishing lodge or to a remote lake in the wilderness.

When someone wants to build a cabin, they ask Grandpa and his great big Otter to haul the lumber to their building site.

Grandpa's airplane is tough and likes to do difficult jobs.

Whenever he goes by with a heavy load, we always say...

"There goes Grandpa."

Grandpa and his airplane work very hard, but sometimes they just want to play. Whenever they want to play, we get to go with them. It is always fun when we get to go flying with Grandpa in his airplane, because

then we can say...

"Let's go

Grandpa!"

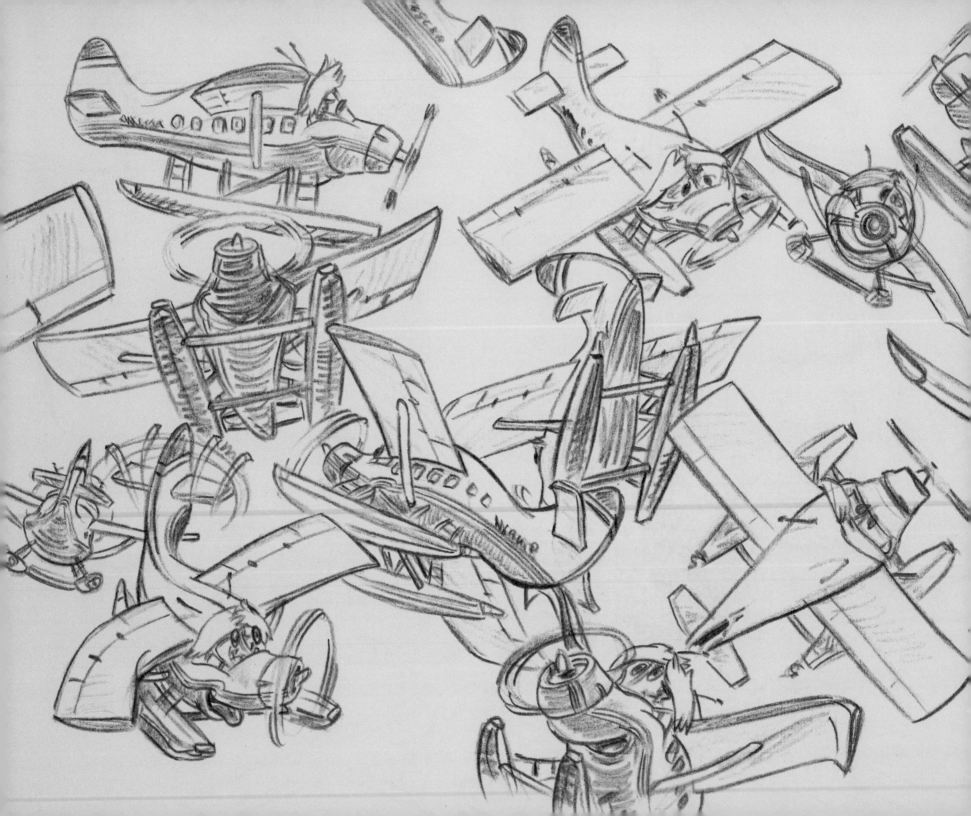